D1568541

✦ Scarlet ✦

Dear Scarlet,

You are *everything* to me! From your smile to your laugh to your giggles and toes, I simply can't imagine life without you. Here's a story to help you understand just how precious you are— and what Everything really means.

Love,

"Scarlet,
did you know you're
my Everything?"
said Big Fox one
evening.

"You tell me all the time!" said Scarlet.
"But what *is* Everything?"

"Oh, Everything is the best thing you could be. It's every new *flower* that blooms in spring."

"And every drop of *rain* that cools the summer."

"It's what it feels like to ride down the longest *hill* in the world. "

"Or to float up to the highest clouds in the *sky*."

"Everything is *warmer* than the softest penguin in the snow."

"And **stronger**
than the tallest
llama in the jungle."

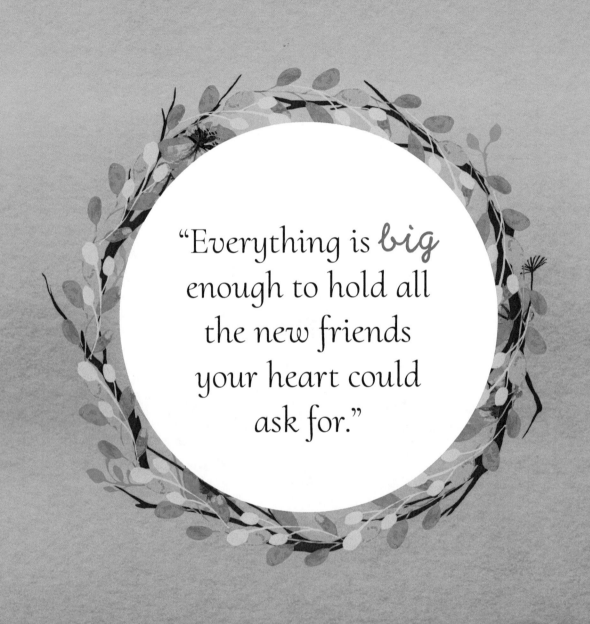

"Everything is *big* enough to hold all the new friends your heart could ask for."

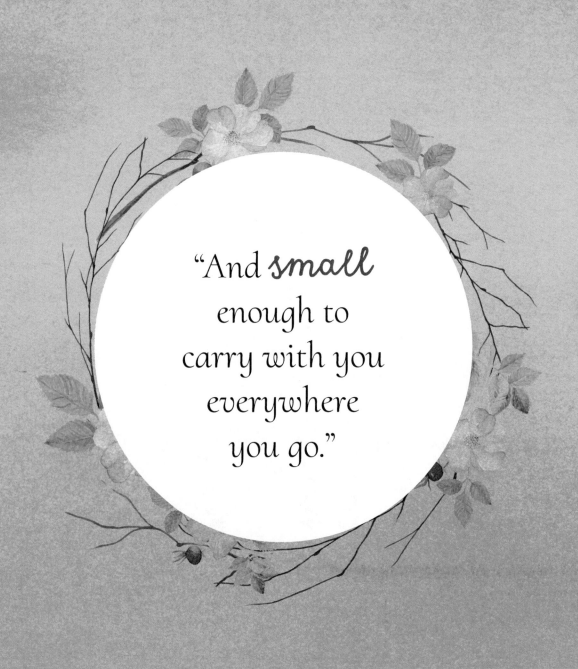

"And *small*
enough to
carry with you
everywhere
you go."

"Everything means,
'I love you with all
my heart.' On your
happy days . . ."

"...and on your *hard* days."

"And it means I will *always* be there during the long, long nights."

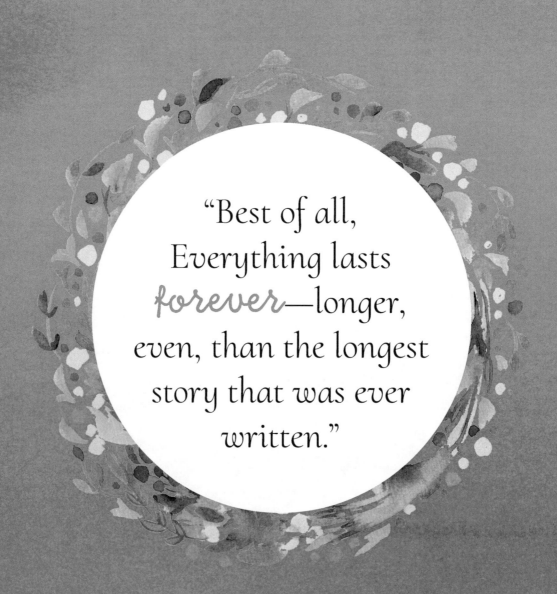

"Best of all,
Everything lasts
forever—longer,
even, than the longest
story that was ever
written."

"Wow," breathed
Scarlet. There
was a comforting
silence.

Then Scarlet whispered, "If Everything means all that, then *you're my Everything, too.*"

Dearest Scarlet, you are my Everything in so many ways! Here are just a few:

Made in United States
North Haven, CT
06 July 2022

21017080R10020